# HIGH
# HEAT

# HIGH
# HEAT

Andrew *Karre*

MINNEAPOLIS

Darby Creek
A division of Lerner Publishing Group, Inc.
241 First Avenue North
Minneapolis, MN 55401 U.S.A.

Website address: www.lernerbooks.com

The images in this book are used with the permission of:
© Kelpfish/Dreamstime.com, p. 109; © iStockphoto.com/
Jill Fromer, p. 112 (banner background); © iStockphoto.
com/Naphtalina, pp. 112, 113, 114 (brick wall background).
Front Cover: © Erik Isakson/CORBIS.
Back Cover: © Kelpfish/Dreamstime.com.

Main body text set in Janson Text 12/17.5.
Typeface provided by Adobe Systems.


Library of Congress Cataloging–in–Publications Data

Karre, Andrew (Andrew Wade), 1978–
    High heat / by Andrew Karre.
        p.   cm. — (Travel team)
    ISBN 978–0–7613–8322–2 (lib. bdg. : alk. paper)
    [1. Baseball—Fiction.]  I. Title.
PZ7.K1495Hig 2012
[Fic]—dc23                           2011032695


Manufactured in the United States of America
1—BP—12/31/11

FOR "STEP AND THROW."

"The way a team plays as a whole determines its success. You may have the greatest bunch of individual stars in the world, but if they don't play together, the club won't be worth a dime."

—BABE RUTH

# CHAPTER 1

[Begin recorded counseling session.]

*Doctor Blanc: How do you feel, Seth?*

Seth Carter: Have you ever woken up after falling asleep on your arm? You know that feeling that your arm isn't really yours? Like it's attached, but not totally under control? Well, that's kinda how my left arm's felt ever since the surgery when I was fifteen.

No, that's not quite true. If I'm really honest with myself, my left arm hasn't been all mine since I was ten or so. That's when my dad first built the practice mound. He built it regulation, you know? 60 feet, 6 inches from the front of the rubber to the back tip of home plate. 10 inches higher than home plate . . .

Am I boring you with these statistics, Doc? No? Because I could go all SportsCenter on you if I'm not careful. WHIP. ERA. OBPS. RBI. ERA. WAR.

When I think back, I knew these numbers—the dimensions, the stats—like most kids knew their phone numbers.

Of course, I didn't throw off the mound when I was ten. Little League mounds are something like 45 feet. Funny, I really don't know that measurement. It never really mattered, I guess. 60 feet, 6 inches, .4 seconds. That's where I was headed.

# CHAPTER 2

*Was it hard to leave Kansas City and come to Nevada?*

We moved to Vegas for the last bit of my rehab, so not really. I was going nuts by then. Everybody I knew—all my so-called friends— were doing their own things. Baseball, mainly—and I couldn't do that, obviously.

Actually, it wasn't so obvious. You know, you don't get a cast for Tommy John surgery. Sure, you get a brace for a couple months, but eventually that comes off and you look normal. I remember that day, when I didn't need the brace.

I had my last therapy session, and the tech—Rick—said I was clear to ditch the brace.

"You're officially done with the robo-arm, kid," Rick said.

"Really?" I must have sounded like an idiot. I mean, I knew I wouldn't be in the brace forever, but to get through those horrible rehab sessions, I kinda just put my head down and stopped thinking.

"Yep," he said, and he shook my hand. For a moment it felt like my arm. "But don't get carried away. You're still a few months away from pitching workouts." He was still gripping my hand, though. He wasn't being dainty about it either. It felt good.

Then I felt a hand on my shoulder. "We know." That was my dad.

Suddenly it didn't feel like my arm any more.

After that, Dad drove us by the park where he knew a summer league team would be practicing. We stopped and got out. It was a practice day. I knew a few of the guys who were warming up with long toss near the edge of the parking lot. One of them recognized me. "Yo, Seth. How's it going?" and he threw the ball my way. Totally cool. Friendly. Normal. Just a way of saying good to see you back on the field. Back in the game.

I caught the ball. Left handed, of course. Then I passed the ball over to my right and there was that hand on my shoulder again.

I know Dad was just reminding me. Heck, I might have thrown it without thinking. How lame would that be? To screw up my rehab five minutes after I got out of that stupid brace? I know what he meant by it. But still.

Anyway, I put the ball back in my left hand. "It's good," I yelled back. "It's good. Arm's almost normal. I'll see you—" and with my left arm I underhanded the ball to him. It rolled to a stop at his feet.

. . .

Anyway, yeah. Leaving KC. I don't know about you, but I can only play so much Xbox. Moving to Vegas was great. Just great.

# CHAPTER 3

*Can you tell me more about the decision to have the procedure?*

"Procedure." That makes it sound so . . . I don't know . . . routine. Simple.

Do you know what Tommy John— sorry, I should say *ulnar collateral ligament reconstruction*—surgery is?

The surgeon slices open your good arm, cuts a bit of ligament out, and then somehow they weave that ligament into the one in the screwed-up arm. Heck of a procedure, if you ask me. A miracle.

But you're a doctor, so you probably knew that. You asked about the decision to do it.

Looking back on it, I think I know when my dad got the idea for the surgery. It was after a summer league game. I'd pitched seven innings against a bunch of U17 guys. I'd struck out ten. No runs, just two hits. But it was a quality team, and they'd worked some deep counts. I'd had to work to get those outs. Even then, I was baseball-smart enough to know that it would be better for me if I could pitch to contact a bit more—count on my defense to turn grounders into outs. But the infield behind me was Swiss cheese, and the offense had repaid my shutout with a one-run lead. So, pitching to contact? Not so much.

I'd mixed in a lot of curves with my two-seamer, so I was already pretty sore when I faced the potential final out in the seventh. Kid before him had reached first on an error, took second on a passed ball (did I mention my catcher was worthless?), and then stole this standing up (yes, that worthless). Still, two outs, so the guy at bat was going to have to get a hit. And he gave it a shot, I'll say that. He must have fouled off five pitches before the count went full when my curve missed the corner. Stupid catcher called curve again, but I shook him off until he squared up for a fastball. Enough of this crap. Dude was going to strike out on this pitch or he was going to homer.

I never lost a game for that team, despite my teammates' best efforts, so you figure out what happened on that last pitch.

I remember lining up for post-game handshakes, rubbing my elbow, and seeing my dad talking to our coach. I couldn't make out all he said, but he was pointing at the pitch counter he always kept on him at games.

Twenty minutes later, we were in the car and I was still rubbing my elbow.

"I can't believe he left you out there for a hundred twenty pitches," my dad said. "Well don't worry. I gave him an earful. That's never happening again— Hey, is something wrong with your arm?"

. . .

The thing is, there wasn't anything wrong—I mean, I was sore. But that's it. My dad wasn't convinced, though. I saw this doctor he'd found online the next week. Two weeks later I was having surgery.

I remember sitting at the kitchen table together after the doctor said surgery was a good option. My dad had been happy.

"They're so good at this surgery now, Seth," he said. "Completely different from my day." He gestured to his laptop. "I've been reading about it. Lots of guys throw harder after the surgery. People look for a good excuse to get this surgery now. You're lucky. This could end up being a big break for you."

I nodded, but something wasn't right. We'd seen one doctor. No second opinion. And the doc never said, "Yes, sir, that ligament is torn." He just did the exam, talked to my dad, and scheduled the procedure. The surgery.

# CHAPTER 4

*Tell me about how your father approached baseball.*

You should know about my dad. He had a cannon for an arm too. It showed up a little later—not until high school. But to hear people talk about it, and from what I've seen from the yearbooks, he made the most of those last two years. Records. Championships. Local newspapers talking about full rides. The whole deal.

You know where this is going, right? All right, let me eliminate a possibility or two. No, he didn't get my mom knocked up. She was thirty when I was born, and they met way after high school. No, he didn't fall in with the wrong crowd, get blitzed on prom night, and kill his date in some car wreck. Are you crazy? That's TV.

No, it was just a twinge in his elbow after that last game. Then, over the summer, he did some goofing around on the mound. "Just to keep loose," he'll say if you press him. The twinge became an ache. The ache became a visit to a doctor, then an orthopedic surgeon. You can probably fill in the rest.

Or maybe not. Reconstructive elbow surgery—called "Tommy John" surgery after the Yankee pitcher who had it in the seventies—is as routine as Botox these days. It's like a ligament assembly line. I exaggerate, but only a bit. Back then, it was a little less mainstream. Some surgeons weren't exactly perfect at it. And after eighteen months of rehab, everyone could see that Dad's doc certainly wasn't. Oh, his elbow stopped hurting. The surgery was a "success." Dad had no pain, good range of motion. But the zip on his fastball? Zapped. The bite on his curve? Bit the dust. Sure, he still had a changeup that scouts had called "mature" and "every bit as potent as his fastball" before the surgery, but the thing about an off-speed pitch is it only works if there's a possibility of an on-speed pitch. And for my dad, there never was again.

He tried to pull a Rick Ankiel and convert to the outfield, but his heart wasn't in hitting, and—why am I bothering with this? You're probably picturing Kevin Costner playing my dad in some movie. Long story short, he moved on, went to school, got a job as a contractor, house, family, kids, divorce, et cetera. And now you're up to date.

# CHAPTER 5

*Other than your teammates on the Roadrunners, did you tell the kids you met when you moved that you were a ballplayer? A pitcher?*

Do you remember the first time you realized you were really good at something? Like, better than everyone else without even making an effort? Maybe you've never had that feeling. (Don't feel too sorry for yourself. It's overrated.)

Anyway, when you discover you're really good and people recognize it, you become that thing. Just like your hair is brown and your eyes are blue.

And it helped that baseball was the family game. We all played. My two older sisters played T-ball, softball, the whole deal. Even my mom played in a softball league before my parents split up. (The girls all avoided the family curse and became position players.)

So what else could I tell people?

. . .

There was this party right after we moved in. It was at Trip Costas' place. Freaking huge house—his dad's a famous singer. At that point I'd been doing workouts with the team for a week or so. They all knew I was a pitcher and that it would be a few weeks before I was cleared to pitch again. I never had to say anything to the team. Coach had explained everything, I guess. Almost everyone had been friendly enough.

Anyway, there were a few Runners at the party—Trip, of course, plus Nick, Sho, Nellie, and Darius. Maybe a couple other guys. The rest were kids from high schools around Vegas. Lots of girls.

We were mostly hanging around the pool, listening to Trip's band play. I was hanging close to Nick, trying to catch people's names.

There was this one girl. She was gorgeous, I'm not going to lie. I kinda couldn't believe it when she just walked up and introduced herself.

"Misha."

"Seth," I stuttered.

Then she actually sat down on the edge of the pool and patted the space next to her. She wanted me to sit. "I haven't seen you around. I'm guessing you're on the team with Trip and Nick, right?" she said. Her feet skimmed the water.

"Yeah, I'm a pitching for the Runners—or I will be when"—I held up my elbow like it would explain everything—"my arm, um, my elbow heals." I think I concluded with something extra lame like, "Looking forward to helping the team."

"Cool," she said. "But let's not talk about baseball. Trip hates it when his parties turn into team meetings," and then she winked at me. "So where are you going to school in the fall?"

I knew I was enrolled somewhere—a North or South something High. It had been such an afterthought for Dad and me that I couldn't think of the name. "Uh, South Jefferson I think it's called?"

She smiled. "Maybe you mean North Jackson?"

"Yeah, that's the one."

"Cool. I go to Vegas Central." I tried not to look disappointed. "So what else are you into? I mean other than baseball."

I stuttered again, "Uh, well, I just moved here, so . . ." Why was it such a hard question? I banged my heels on the edge of the pool.

The only thing that saved me was when a softball landed six feet away in the pool, splashing us both.

Misha looked up toward the top of the hill overlooking the pool and shook her head.

"Where'd that come from?" I asked.

She pointed. "Nick and his boys. They always do this. It drives Trip nuts."

Another softball landed in the pool, followed by Nick yelling, "Hey, rookie! Seth! Get your skinny butt up here!"

Misha stood up. She reached down and gave me her hand. She pulled me to my feet and said, "You'd better go." She glanced over her shoulder and did this half laugh, half snort thing that was weirdly hot. "They're your teammates. I know how that is. But give me a call sometime. Nick's got my number."

"Um, thanks. I will. It was good— I mean, nice to meet you, Misha." I didn't know what else to do, so I stuck out my hand.

She smiled and then shook it.

Nick yelled from the hill, "Seth, are you shaking her hand?"

Darius joined in. "Man, don't shake her hand. Don't they teach you anything in Kansas City? You need me to draw you a diagram?"

"Grow up, Darius," she singsonged back. To me she said, "See you later." And then she headed back toward the house. I just stared.

I never did get her number from Nick. I'm sure he would have given it to me, though.

. . .

I did go up the hill. Nick had turned Trip's pitching machine so they could launch balls at the huge pool three hundred feet down the hill. He'd also loaded it with rag softballs. "Bigger splash, less bruising," he explained.

Nick handed me a bat and took my drink. "Step up to the plate, bro."

And I did. It turns out that launching fly balls into Trip Costa's ridiculously huge pool is a Roadrunner rite of passage. Runners had been doing it since Trip's oldest brother was on the team ten years ago. The pool house had the dents to prove it.

And it was fun. Especially once I got the knack and found my range.

"Dude, you're a natural," said Nick after I dropped three straight into the deep end.

A few kids were sitting around the pool near where I'd sat with Misha. "Heads up," screamed Darius. Then the pitch came and I dropped a towering fly ball six feet from the edge of the pool. Everybody scattered.

Nick and Darius fell over laughing.

Yep, I was a ballplayer.

# CHAPTER 6

*Do you still admire professional baseball players? Would you still like to be one?*

You know who I probably would have played like if things had been different? Pete Rose. Yeah, he's the crazy old guy who shows up on Sports Center every once in a while. Fat dude. Ugly shirts. Trying to make a buck on autographs or whatever. But when I was rehabbing I had a lot of time to watch ESPN Classic. To read books. Turns out Pete Rose the ballplayer was hardcore. Headfirst slide into first base? No problem. Take out the catcher to score from second on a single? Sign him up. Dude was hard as nails, and he just plain loved to play the game. And play it hard.

That's me. That was me. I was old-school even in T-ball.

There's this video my dad used to show people of me in first grade playing T-ball. I whacked the ball into the left-field gap, and by the time the kids got it together I was rounding second.

"Hold up, Seth!" You can hear somebody's dad at third base trying to keep me from turning the corner. I blew by him. Somehow, the catcher ended up with the ball as I was about ten feet from home. He was as surprised as I was.

"Slide, Seth!" my dad was yelling. I think he knew what I was going to do before I did.

The poor kid at the plate seemed to understand a split second later. He took a giant step away from the plate and held out his glove and the ball like he was offering them to me.

You can hear the thunk as I knocked the ball and the glove off his hand as I crossed home.

It's not on the video, but I'm pretty sure they called me out for dangerous play or some crap like that. Didn't matter. Even then I knew it was the right way to play the game.

· · ·

After the surgery, things were different. I'm not saying Dad told me to play different. He never said a word. Like I said before. It's not like that between us. Only, there was a game right after I was cleared to play without any restrictions—probably my first game for the Roadrunners—where I was really feeling it at the plate for the first time since the operation. It just felt fun again, no other way to say it.

Anyway, I ripped one into the gap, and as I was coming into second I just had a sense this was more than a double. So I kept running. Slid hard into third, just under the tag, and sent the third baseman flying. Guy landed on me like a ton of bricks and it hurt like hell, but I was safe. When I saw he'd bobbled the ball a bit, the third-base coach had to scream "don't even think about it" to keep me from trying to score. Like I said. Pete Rose. I was dirty, my pants were torn, and my right arm was bleeding. And I was truly happy for the first time in eighteen months.

I think I scored on the next play. I pitched another couple innings. Didn't bat again, but I'm pretty sure we won. Good times, right?

And Dad was happy, I guess, after the game. We went out, did the pizza thing with a few of the guys. He was pretty quiet, but I was pumped. I don't think I really noticed much beyond how good it felt to have played on instinct again. But when we got back home, there was bill from the hospital in the mailbox, along with all the normal bills and whatever. That wasn't a surprise. The hospital bills had been coming every month for almost two years. Insurance doesn't cover an elective Tommy John surgery, so Dad was paying monthly.

Dad just stared at it for a couple minutes. Then he got the calculator and the checkbook from on top of the refrigerator. For a long time, the only sound at the kitchen table was him punching the keys on that calculator.

You know Las Vegas is a lousy place to be a contractor, right?

I couldn't pitch the next day, so I spent two hours with the pitching machine working on my sacrifice bunts.

I was officially just a pitcher now. No more sliding into anything.

. . .

Wait, I know you're about to ask another question. But I want to say one more thing about how being a pitcher is different. When you pitch, you're all alone, you know? It's all you. You and your thoughts. You and whatever's in your head. I think that part was always a problem for me when I was just a pitcher. The head part.

# CHAPTER 7

*But there were benefits to focusing on pitching, right? You weren't just any pitcher. I've read the articles from the Kansas City paper. You were extraordinary.*

Sure.

I mean, yes, after the rehab was done. I threw hard—harder than I did before. And my pitches had filthy movement.

And I said my arm didn't feel like my own—and it didn't—but it didn't feel bad.

It felt tight and strong. It still felt like the weapon I knew I had when I was twelve. Now it just felt like it had been specially tuned up.

I remember the first practice with the Roadrunners after I was cleared to throw 100 percent off the mound. I'd been with the team for a few weeks, but it had just been BP and conditioning drills. The other guys were nice enough, but it was like they were waiting to see what the big deal was. And I was bored out of my skull. So anyway, I was scheduled to throw an intersquad scrimmage. Roadrunners come ready for those. Kids bring their A games. I was psyched, you might say.

I started in the bottom of the first. Got right down to business. Didn't want to keep the guys waiting.

First pitch: high and outside. Ball one, but it felt good.

Second pitch: down and in, ball two. I remember that one *sounded* good. I mean when it hit Nick's glove.

Third pitch: down the middle. Sammy swung, but he was hopelessly late. Strike one.

Fourth pitch: same location, same result.
Now the coaches were paying attention.
Even Carson stopped playing catch to watch.
Somebody had the radar gun out now. Ninety
and more.

Fifth pitch: do I even need to tell you?

. . .

At 0-2 on the third batter, Nick called time
and ran out to the mound.

"What's up?" I asked.

"Nothing, just wanted to chat," he said as
he took off his mitt.

"Chat?"

"Well, to be honest, my left hand hurts
and I need a break. I didn't think you'd
take me seriously if signaled changeup, so
I figured this was the best way to get some
relief."

I just stared at him.

Nick smiled and hit me on the right
shoulder. "Just kidding, rookie. Welcome to
the Roadrunners. It's gonna be a heck of a

season. Between you and Carson, we're going to light up this league."

I threw two more innings. No runs, no hits. Seven Ks. I mixed in some breaking pitches with the heater to keep the guys guessing. I even threw a changeup. Nick dropped it, and the batter swung like five minutes early.

# CHAPTER 8

*The first game of the season was a couple
days after that, correct? What happened?*

[Long pause.]

# CHAPTER 9

*Seth, I know this is hard for you, so I'll just say it. That was the game when the player was injured. What was it like when you hit him?*

[Pause.]

OK. I hit the kid in the head. That's what you wanted me to say, right?

It was the top of the third. I'd been toying with everyone in their lineup, and then their ninth batter comes up, and he works a full count. He had to foul off eight pitches, but he managed it. If I'm honest, I was probably getting tired at that point. I just wanted out of the inning.

Nick showed splitter, and I waved it off. I waved off everything until he showed fastball. I did my thing, my windup, and it was like before the surgery. The batter was either going to strike out or plant it in the bleachers. But then I released, and it immediately felt wrong. It got away from me somehow.

[Pause.]

I can still hear the noise. It's worse than the sound of a ball hitting a helmet. I just clipped the bottom of his helmet as he tried to twist out of the way. The ball got him right at the base of the head.

So there was this smack too, like when you hit your palm with your fist. But much louder.

He was out before he hit the ground. He didn't even catch himself. Just landed flat on his face. I could see the dirt in his mouth, and his eyes were rolled back in his head.

But it was the sound that stays with me. I've never heard quiet like that. I mean, it *wasn't* quiet. Not really. Nick was down on his knees yelling at the kid. The trainer was out right away, and there were coaches and umpires and whatever gathered all around. I'm sure they were all yelling, but I couldn't hear anything but that smack.

When you see a headshot like that on TV, the pitcher always squats down on the mound and looks at the dirt, like he wants to disappear into the dirt. I always thought that was weird. Now I don't. You feel like dirt. I wanted to disappear.

# CHAPTER 10

*Can you talk about how things went when you pitched again?*

I finished the inning. I know that's not what you asked, but I want to say that. Next batter grounded to short on the first pitch. When I hit the dugout, Coach told me good inning, but I was done.

"Those were quality innings, Seth. You're going to be a big help this season. But let's not rush things. Gotta have you fresh for Cuba."

I didn't complain. Heck, I still thought it was a fluke thing then too.

. . .

So, when I pitched again? Well, it was days before I pitched again, you know that, right? I mean, starters only go every five days, max.

Anyway, I have a routine between starts. Dad helped me develop it, big surprise. First day after a start is key. I don't touch a baseball. I've got a recovery, stretching, and strength-training routine. I did that, and then I went for a run. The run is key for me. My dad would normally come out on the run with me, and we'd talk over the game. Or we'd talk about the next start. But Dad was picking up all sorts of overtime, so he was still sleeping when I headed out to the practice facility. Too hot to run outside.

Honestly, I was kinda looking forward to doing my run alone with my iPod and then—I don't know—going to the mall or something brainless. I needed to get that sound out of my head.

The team had the day off, so I figured I'd have the place to myself. And I did, except for Carson was already on one of the treadmills when I got there. He was pitching our next game.

He had his earbuds in, so I just nodded at him and started on the other treadmill. I set a moderate pace and just tried to zone out. But you know how when see a horror movie that's got one scene that's just completely screwed up? And you can't get it out of your head even though it's completely freaking you out? The sound was like that. It was like *The Hostel* or *Saw*—one of those crazy gory movies. Just the sound and that kid's lifeless body dropping.

Carson actually snapped me out of my own private horror movie. I heard his treadmill beep when his run was over, and I noticed him hitting pause on his iPhone out of the corner of my eye.

He said something. I didn't quite catch it. I pulled out my earbuds and hit the stop button on the treadmill.

"I said 'nice scar, Carter,'" he repeated. I looked at my elbow. "Was it worth it?" Then he walked away.

I hadn't told anyone in Vegas, you understand? No one should have known, but somehow he knew.

. . .

I guess I didn't really answer your question, did I? There were no more real games scheduled before the Havana Invitational, so we had a couple more intersquads set up before we flew down. I didn't pitch to real batters before the tournament.

# CHAPTER *11*

*Tell me about the trip to Cuba. That must have been very exciting for you and your teammates. I understand this tournament was a very big honor for the Roadrunners.*

Yeah, I guess. Coach wanted us to stay totally focused. "They call this the Goodwill Series," he told us a week or so before we left. "But make no mistake, gentlemen: this is just like any other series. Somebody will win. And somebody will lose. Goodwill doesn't really enter into it as far as you're concerned, Roadrunners."

He showed us some film of the Cuban team, told us they played hard—played "desperate," he said. "You might be tempted to think this trip is a couple hours of baseball interrupting your Caribbean vacation, but I can assure you this is the best U17 team in Cuba. They will hand you your jockstraps if your minds are on the beach."

And we took it seriously. Bryce Harper played in this tournament before he went number one in the draft. Playing well against a Cuban team was a surefire way to get noticed by scouts and to end up in the mock drafts that were all over the Internet. When I think about it, this tournament was what clinched Las Vegas for my dad and me. I remember when we made the decision.

"Tampa Bay. I've got a good feeling about Tampa Bay." This was the first thing I said to my dad one morning after he picked me up from a physical therapy session. It was one of those sessions where I had to sit with my arm in a tub of ice water for an hour. So I'd been over this packet of scouting reports and forum postings about the under-seventeen baseball scene in south Florida. That and some careful reporting in a certain special issue of *Sports Illustrated* had me leaning pretty hard toward Florida by the time my tub session was done.

All my dad said was, "Florida, eh? Might want to consider this before you make up your mind." He handed me his phone. There was a text from Coach Harris on the screen:

"Can confirm RRs' place in the 2013 Goodwill Series in Havana. Looking 4ward 2 seeing Seth pitch in Cuba."

I handed Dad his phone. "Viva Las Vegas" was all I said. Dad called the realtor when we got home.

. . .

Still, despite Coach's lecture, some of the guys were thinking about beaches and bars that didn't card. It showed. We were practicing like crap. You know, the crap practices probably helped me in a weird way. I mean, I wasn't concentrating enough to get into that zone where I'd hit the kid. My stuff was good enough to get scrimmage outs on guys who were thinking bikinis, not breaking balls. No reason to really let fly, so no danger. No chance of hearing that sound again. So I think everyone thought I was OK.

Except maybe Nick, I guess. I think he knew something was up. He gave me a ride back from practice one day, and out of nowhere he said, "You're not still rattled by that one that got away from you last week, are you?"

"What? No way," I stammered. "I haven't given it a thought," I lied.

"Good to hear, because I know you've been taking a little bit off your fastballs. I mean, nobody else is going to notice—not the way they've been practicing—but me," he flexed his left hand, "well, I notice because my hand isn't numb after I catch you."

"Yeah, well, no need to go 110 percent in practice. I mean, Nick, you know I'll bring it when it counts. In Cuba." I must have sounded so defensive.

"Easy, Seth. No worries. I don't doubt you. You've just got to know you don't have to do it all yourself. You don't have to strike out everybody. Pitch to contact. Make 'em hit grounders. You've got a solid infield. We'll win if you just hit your spots. You don't have to throw it by everybody. It's not one on one."

Thinking back, I realize Nick knew me better than I knew myself. At the time I just nodded. We talked about something else for the rest of the ride to my house.

We still practiced like Little Leaguers the days before the tournament, but at that point I think it was nerves more than bikinis.

After one lousy practice, Coach must have decided to let the captains—Nellie and Carson—let us have it. And they kind of did. It was a lot of the usual crap guys say to each other in situations like that.

Carson threw in a little extra for me: "We've all got to have our heads screwed on for this tournament. Some of us have a lot riding on this. Not all of us can count on special help." Then he looked at me. "Right, Tommy John?"

# CHAPTER *12*

*So Carson knew about your elbow operation. So what? Why would he care?*

You got to know about Carson. He's used to getting what he wants, and he doesn't like to be shown up.

I'm not saying he's not good—he is. He's got an effective fastball and a couple strong secondary pitches. But he gets rattled. And it turns out nothing rattles him more than competition. The other starters on the team are good, but they don't want to be The Ace, so they never threatened Carson. That first day I threw in a game and the radar gun showed 90s, he felt threatened.

Ninety miles per hour is a funny thing for a pitcher. The difference between eighty-nine and ninety-one miles per hour is way more than two, and Carson knows that. He did not like watching me from the wrong side of that divide.

The only way for him to fix his head was to screw with mine. And Carson is a smart guy. He could see the scars on my elbow. He reads the same baseball blogs I do. He's heard about guys getting this surgery for shady reasons. Google "elective Tommy John" if you don't believe me. And he could Google my name and see lots of Kansas City coverage of my games when I was fourteen and fifteen. Then he'd see almost two years of nothing at all about Seth Carter's freakish fastball. It wouldn't take a genius.

The other thing you've got to know about Carson is that he's loaded—or his family is.

His dad is obsessed with making sure we have the best. When the team played in a wooden-bat tournament early in the season, Carson's dad bought a pile of Sam Bats—the crazy expensive maple bats pros use. Carson's dad took care of the team, but the trade-off was that Carson acted like he owned the place sometimes—and he kinda did.

I think that's why the coaches tolerated it when he did his bit with the fancy new hundred-mile-per-hour-proof helmets his dad bought for the team right before Cuba.

We were scheduled for a film session—yeah, we have a video setup at the practice facility. I'm sure Carson's dad paid for it.

Anyway, I was sitting with Sammy, talking about who knows what, when Carson came in.

"All right, listen up, gentlemen." Carson stood in front of the huge flat-screen TV. "I've got a little announcement before the coaches get here and we get down to business.

"We've all seen the news about concussions and all the other crap that can mess up your life when you take a heater to the head." Then he stepped aside from in front of the screen and pressed the remote.

A sequence of famous bean balls pulled from SportsCenter highlights played. It was just one headshot after another. I don't know if he edited out all the other sound, but all I heard was ball hitting helmet. Ball hitting bone.

"So, it's a bad scene, right?" Carson continued, looking right at me. "Well, my dad just got us these new . . ."

I don't know exactly what he said next because, I knocked over my chair running out of the room. I barely made the hallway before I puked out my lunch.

I did hear Carson say, "What's the matter, Tommy John?"

# CHAPTER *13*

*Did you pitch again before the Cuba tournament?*

Just workouts and simulated stuff. Batting practice. Nothing where it was really game-on, you know?

My head was pretty thoroughly screwed at that point. Even I didn't know how much, though. Maybe it was the new helmets or Nick's constant refrain: "pitch to contact; trust the defense." Either way, I was able to pitch well enough in practice that no one saw a problem.

Mostly, I spent time with Nick, the other pitchers, and Wash, looking at whatever film and scouting reports we had on their hitters.

"Their three and four hitters are brothers," Wash told us. "Really quality power hitters. Lots of plate discipline, but when they get a pitch to hit, they're not afraid to swing. Their offense is built on production from these two—extra bases, home runs." He looked at me and at Carson. "You've got to remember to trust your defense. You make these two settle for ground balls and don't let them work long at bats, and we'll be OK."

# CHAPTER 14

*Tell me about when you found out you'd be starting the first game in Cuba.*

Coach waited until the day we left to post the starters, and when he did, Carson had a fit. I have to say, Wash managed Carson's bruised ego perfectly.

"Wait, Coach is starting game one with the head—"

"Ease off, Carson," Wash said. "Use your brain. We've got three games here, and there's every chance we'll need to win the third to take this series. Seth's coming off an injury and doesn't have the base conditioning you have. If he gets an extra day of rest, he can be available for relief innings if we need him in game three. Coach and I just assumed you could handle the short rest in such an important tournament if we need you. We weren't wrong, were we, Carson? Are you not up to the challenge, Carson?"

That shut him up.

That was also when we found out the Roadrunners would be making a goodwill gift to the Cuban team. They'd be the lucky recipients of a complete set of Rawlings S100 helmets—the same ones we were now using. Courtesy of Carson's dad, of course. It should have made me feel better.

There was one other announcement from the coaches. Dave was sick and wouldn't be able to make the trip. We'd have to travel with fewer pitchers than we normally would. No pressure.

# CHAPTER *15*

*Seth, tell me about the first game—*
*everything you can remember. Don't think*
*about it; just tell me what you remember.*

So the first game was the day after we
arrived. We'd landed in Havana pretty early,
and Coach let everyone have the rest of the
day off as long as we were in our rooms by ten.
The plan worked. A lot of guys must have got
the beach thing out of their systems. We had
a BP session the next morning, and while I

was playing long toss with Shotaro I watched Nick, Sammy, and Darius have a mini home-run derby. We looked sharp. The practice rust was gone. Even I felt good.

We finished our workouts, and Nick sat next to me on the bus back to the hotel.

"You feelin' it, Seth?" He took a deep breath and stretched his arms. "Opportunity, man. We are going to light these guys up." Then he got serious. "Just locate, Seth. Trust your infield. You don't have to strike everyone out. We don't need Stephen Strasburg. Have fun and keep the ball down. We'll win this thing."

I just nodded. I tried to remember when "having fun" had been a priority for me in baseball.

. . .

The game was at seven—I guess so people could come after work. And man, were there people. I don't know much about Cuba, but I know people there don't generally live as well as they do in the States. But that stadium was major league, and it was major-league full by game time.

We were home for game one, so I got a taste of the home fans right away. It's not like they booed us when we took the field after the national anthems. No, they were polite enough. It's just that they went nuts for the Cuban team's lineup. You'd have thought everyone in the stands was related to them the way they cheered. The Cubans actually looked a little scared.

Before we went out, Coach told Nick and me, "Don't hold anything back in the beginning. These kids are as nervous as you are—if not more. If you can dominate right away, we might get into their heads. Make 'em doubt they've got a chance."

"Got it, Coach," I said.

Nick just nodded. As we jogged out, though, he said, "Don't be afraid to pitch to contact. Coach is right, of course. Dominate or whatever. But remember what Wash said, too. You still gotta trust your infield. Make 'em hit grounders, and the guys behind you will take care of the rest."

I heard him, and I didn't hear him. Can you blame me? Which would you rather do? Pitch to contact? Or dominate?

. . .

Fortunately, in the first inning, domination was pretty easy.

Nick showed heater on the first pitch, and I blew it by the guy. He fought off the second pitch, and I rung him up with my changeup on the next pitch.

Pretty much the same story with the next guy.

The first two hitters looked like classic leadoff guys—high OBP guys with speed. We knew, of course, that their third and fourth hitters were power guys. Well, I was in the perfect position to face a power hitter. Two outs and no men on. I was feelin' it—just like Nick said.

My first fastball was inside and a little low, and he took it for a ball. Dude had a good eye. I went right back at him on the next pitch, and this one was on the money, but somehow he managed to get the bat on it. He was a little under it, so it was higher than it was far. Still, Darius had to backpedal before he made the grab. Dude definitely had a good eye and an even better swing. Not even Sammy would have gotten around on that pitch—and he was easily our best hitter.

Still, three up, three down.

In our half of the inning, things went a little better for our top three. Nellie singled up the middle. Their pitcher had a really slow delivery, so he stole second right away. Trip struck out, but the catcher muffed the ball and Nellie went to third. Nick hit a textbook sac fly on the second pitch, and Nellie scored easily. Then the pitcher seemed to settle down, because he made Sammy look silly with his curve. The inning ended with a swinging strikeout.

When I went out for the top of the second, though, I thought something was wrong. Their cleanup hitter looked exactly like their third hitter, except he batted left. I'd known they were brothers from the scouting report, of course, but the resemblance was still eerie—and the switch-hitting thing was just plain crazy.

He had his brother's good eye. My first two pitches were a little off, and he took them without hesitation for 2 and 0. Wash's voice echoed in my head, "Don't let three and four work long at bats." I got him to bite on my curve, and then he punished a fastball that rode a little high. He was a bit late on it, so it went well foul. Still, he probably hit it 350 feet.

Nick showed sinker on the 2-2, and I shook him off. He showed sinker again, and I shook him off again.

He popped put of his crouch and called time.

"Seth, think about this. You don't need to strike this guy out. There's nobody on." He was talking into his glove so nobody else could hear or read lips, but I could see from his eyes that he was pissed. "The only way this guy can hurt you is if he goes deep. Throw the stupid sinker, and let's move on."

I nodded, and he ran back. I wound up, threw, and the batter swung over it by just enough to send it ripping toward short. The infield definitely played fast, and he'd hit it hard, but Trip handled it, and the guy was out at first.

Nick was right. I got ahead of the next two hitters, no problem, and they both went down swinging.

The thing about pitchers is that we feed off of each other. My first two innings were like an invitation to the Cuban hurler: "Hey, wanna do a pitcher's duel?"

In the bottom half of the second he answered "yes." Three up, three down. I think he threw nine pitches. The slow delivery isn't a problem if no one's on base.

Top of the third, I got into a groove with Nick—or at least I started that way. I trusted him to call the game, and the first batter grounded weakly to third on the second pitch, and I rung up the second guy looking. The ninth batter was their pitcher, and he should have been an easy out. And he probably looked like he was. He got a piece of my curve and popped it up near first. Trip waved everybody off and gloved it easily at the edge of the outfield. Somehow, though, the pitcher caught my eye. He didn't just go through the motions running to first. He hustled, and his helmet popped off the back of his head as he ran. It made a sort of plasticky, hollow clatter as it bounced in the dirt. It was just a regular batting helmet, but to me it sounded like a toy—like one of those pretend helmets they give away to kids at games. No protection at all.

I realized they weren't wearing the new helmets we'd given them. I walked like a zombie back to the dugout. The only thing that snapped me out was Wash handing me my bat—and one of our new helmets.

"Nice inning, Seth. Way to stay with Nick," he said. "Focus on your at bat now. You just move the runner over, you got it? Nothing fancy."

There was a man on first when I got up. Unfortunately, I swung at the first pitch, and their infield turned my weak grounder into a textbook 4-6-3 double play. Their pitcher finished us off by fanning Nellie. I was back out before I had a chance to think.

# CHAPTER *16*

*Let me stop you, Seth. You had a no-hitter going. That must have given you some confidence?*

In the fourth inning? I honestly don't think I noticed. No way any of my teammates were going to say anything.

When I got back out in the fourth, I just wanted to keep following Nick's lead—like I'd never noticed the helmets. Nick's signals were all that was keeping me above water.

I started to chant, "Ground balls; trust the defense. Pitch to contact; have faith in the infield." I must have looked like a schizo out there mumbling to myself. But it was working.

Their leadoff guy swung at two pitches that were outside the zone. Then he only barely managed to check his swing on my changeup. I fielded the weak comebacker and fired to first.

The throw was good, but the first baseman juggled it a bit. He recovered, and the runner was still out, but the little bobble broke my concentration. My chant was fading.

I jammed the number-two hitter with a fastball inside, and he hit it toward third off the handle of his bat. It was a routine grounder, but Nellie didn't field it cleanly. He had to hurry his throw, and he was off target. The runner was safe on the error.

Now the chant and the concentration were gone. And I had to face their three and four now. (But hey, Doc, I still had a no-hitter, right?)

I forced my eyes to focus on Nick's signs. A rational pitcher would have been thinking that a ground ball is a double-play opportunity. That's what Nick was thinking.

I got lucky with the first two pitches. The batter fouled both back. He worked the count to 2–2 by holding off on a couple of outside fastballs.

I swear Nick called for a changeup next. It's what I threw, and it totally fooled the hitter. Unfortunately, it also fooled Nick, and the ball got by him.

His helmet was off in a second and he spun around for the ball. He kicked it in the process, and before he finally got ahold of it, there were runners on first and third.

And in case you're scoring at home, Doc, there was only one out. But I still had a no-hitter.

Nick came out to the mound before the next batter. "Nothing changes, man. Hear me? That was some flukey crap. It's out of our systems, right?" He slapped my arm, but I was totally focused on the total lack of certainty in his voice. Nick wasn't sure.

I had nothing now.

"Settle down, Roadrunners," Wash called from the dugout.

I half hoped to see Coach call for an intentional pass on the cleanup hitter, but he just yelled, "Keep sharp. Look for double play."

I tried to zero in on Nick for the signs, but the runner on first was taking too much lead. I tried to keep him honest with a quick throw to first.

There was no avoiding it, though. My first fastball was high and outside, and the batter didn't flinch. I came inside on the next one and he fouled it off. He did the same for the next three pitches.

It was 1-2. I was ahead on the count, but it didn't feel like it. The batter's face never changed. He showed no strain. Honestly, I thought he was toying with me.

And maybe he was. Just as I was about to start my next pitch he called time and stepped out. He methodically tightened a pair of well-worn batting gloves. Then he stepped back in and fouled off two more pitches.

My nerves were destroyed at this point. All I could remember was that feeling from games back in Kansas City before the surgery. Then I knew I had a Swiss-cheese infield, and I would have to finish this myself. Then I would just have reached back to wherever I kept those extra couple miles per hour and let one go. Two possible outcomes: home run or strikeout. And that's what I did this time.

Except there are three possible outcomes.

I knew the pitch was wrong when I released it. The extra miles per hour were there. The location was not.

This time it got all helmet, and that's probably what saved him.

Still, the batter who had been the picture of power and control ten seconds earlier was now facedown in the dirt. His legs were kicking like crazy.

Looking back, that was probably a good sign. He was OK. In pain, but not unconscious. I didn't take it that way at the time.

Soon there were trainers and the whole deal. And two minutes later, he walked to first and the bases were loaded.

Coach Harris and Nick came to me at the mound. "You got to shake it off, Carter. You've been great all day. Stick with Nick. You can get out of this." Nick was nodding and saying something, but I was in a fog. All I could hear was the sound.

# CHAPTER *17*

*But you did get out of it. They only scored one run in that inning. Something must have worked.*

Pure luck. The five hitter only managed a sac fly. And the infield got ahold of itself on the next guy, and he grounded out to second. Textbook, really.

It made no sense, but we were tied at one, and I still had a no-hitter, technically. Maybe that's why Coach didn't pull me right away. From the outside, it looked like I'd been pitching reasonably efficiently and that I'd been the victim of some weak defense. And we were a little thin in the bullpen with Dave not making the trip. Really, I'd only thrown one bad pitch.

Problem was, it seemed to me like the only pitch I'd thrown.

. . .

Anyway, our guys finally got to their pitcher a bit in our half of the fourth. We got two singles and a walk with no outs to load the bases.

Their pitcher fought back and managed to fan our next two. But then he walked in a run to break the tie.

And then Darius poked a double to the gap in left. It almost broke things wide open for us, but their left fielder limited the damage to two runs with a strong throw back to the infield. I was up with two down and runners on second and third.

Based on what they'd seen from my first at bat, I almost expected them to risk pitching to me rather than load up the bases for Nellie, who'd already shown he could hit their pitcher. Still, Wash yelled from the dugout, "Keep sharp, Carter." I could see in his eyes what he meant. Watch out for the payback pitch.

As I walked toward the box, the only thing that really registered for me was that their cleanup hitter was standing in left field. He hadn't come out the game. Like the rest of the outfield he took several steps in.

# CHAPTER 18

*Was Coach Washington worried the other pitcher might hit you in revenge?*

Duh.

It's not really revenge, though. It's just baseball. I'd plunked their best hitter. It's the pitcher's job to protect his batters. A brushback pitch would have made some sense strategically. There was an open base and two outs. The pitcher could deliver a message and not hurt his team much at all. I know if their pitcher had drilled Sammy and I was on the mound, I'd be looking for the nod from the dugout. For permission to send a message.

And honestly, I wanted him to hit me. As I walked from the on-deck circle, I imagined a pitch somehow hitting my right arm and smashing it. I would feel something then. A broken arm would be *my* arm again.

I knew I would stand in when I got to the box—that I wouldn't jump back from an inside pitch. That was a little comforting.

But I should have known when the outfield played me in that they weren't going to drill me. They must have thought I would be an easy out. The pitcher came right at me with a wicked fastball that caught the corner. I was completely fooled by his changeup on the next pitch. He finished a humiliating at bat by blowing a fastball by me.

I guess they played the situation right. I was an easy out.

# CHAPTER 19

*And just like that you had to pitch again, right?*

Yep.

I don't know what to say. It was a disaster? I got the yips? None of that really covers it, because every ball in the dirt, every fifty-mile-per-hour "fastball" that Nick had to jump for, was a wish granted. The clang of the ball hitting the backstop was a wave of relief compared to that other sound. The sound of ball on helmet. On bone.

I would have loaded the bases in twelve pitches if Nick and Coach hadn't relieved me of the ball after the second walk (and after the first batter I'd walked made it to third standing up on my wild pitches).

It was the first time I'd ever seen Nick speechless. Coach only said, "Make sure Wash gets a look at your arm, Seth." Then he took the ball and put his hand on my shoulder. I think I just nodded and walked toward the dugout.

Funny thing was, the guys had already been ignoring me because of the no-hitter— it's a weird baseball tradition not to sit next to a pitcher during a no-no. I still had that no-hitter, technically, but that's not why they were ignoring me at that point.

None of them had ever seen anything quite like what just happened.

"Let's have a look at that arm, Carter."

Wash. He wasn't ignoring me.

He took my elbow in his huge hands. "Pain?"

I shook my head.

"And you didn't feel a pop?"

Shook it again.

He looked at me for a long a time. "What happened with their cleanup hitter was an accident, Seth. You know that. Heck, *he* knows that. A pitch got away from you. Shake it off, son. Shake it off."

I nodded. I managed to say, "Right, Coach," even though my mouth felt like it was full of sand.

. . .

Shotoro came in for me. Nick and Sho have this kind of telepathy, it seems. They just know how to go after batters as a unit. If anyone could have gotten us out of that inning with the lead intact it, it was them. But I didn't give them much to work with. I'd handed them the top of the Cuban team's order with no outs and runners in scoring position.

Sho managed to strike out the leadoff hitter, but the next guy blooped a single over second base, and one run scored. The next guy managed to get around on a fastball and went deep to right. Fortunately, Darius handled it on the track, so only one more run scored.

Their cleanup hitter stepped in. Something looked different, and it took me a minute to notice.

"Hey, Tommy John, looks like you knocked some sense into that kid." Carson noticed too, from the other end of the bench. The cleanup hitter was wearing one of the new helmets we'd given them.

I didn't say anything. I just watched as the hitter drilled Sho's first pitch to the left-field wall. Two runs scored on his double. The kid tapped his new helmet as he pulled up at second. His teammates all came to the top of the dugout steps and clapped.

Sho managed to induce a grounder to second on the next guy and the inning was over. All things considered, it could have been much worse.

# CHAPTER 20

*No one else was thinking about what
happened to the cleanup hitter, were they,
Seth? No one was blaming you.*

Maybe. But the momentum had swung
away from the Roadrunners, it turned out.

There was a bright spot, I guess. Sho
pitched the rest of the game, and he was
solid.

"Way to attack the corners, bro," I heard
Nick tell him at the end of a clean inning.

"Give me a target, man, and I'll nail," Sho replied.

I was staring at my cleats as they talked. I envied Nick and Sho their easy connection and their effortless confidence. I was jealous of them even as the innings passed and our offense failed to get back the runs I'd allowed. (That's the cruel thing about baseball scoring—even if the runs score after you're relieved, they're still yours if you let them on base.)

In the end, I'd given the Cubans all the runs they'd need. We lost the first game five to four.

# CHAPTER 21

*But it was a three-game series, right?*
*There was still a chance to win.*

Sure. And credit where credit is due. I may think Carson is jerk, but once he knew his game was must-win, he really focused.

I ran into him on my way back to the hotel, standing at the elevator, and I almost turned around to take the stairs—it was only four floors to my room. But he saw me.

"Hey, Seth. Tough break out there. Your stuff was filthy for those first four innings, though," he said. "We'll get it back tomorrow. No worries."

It was just empty babble. Even though I was still in shock, I think, I could tell his mind was elsewhere—on the game tomorrow. He was bouncing on the balls of his feet, like a boxer. He was nervous, but he wasn't scared. He truly didn't have any worries. He wanted the ball tomorrow. Heck, I think he wanted the game to start right now. There was no fear in him, just competitiveness, pure and simple.

We got in the elevator, and as he fidgeted, I tried to remember what it was like to feel that way, to want the ball with the series on the line. I knew I must have, once upon a time.

But I couldn't remember. I only had worries now.

The elevator opened at my floor. "Good luck tomorrow, Carson. They don't have a chance."

He popped out of his zone just as the doors began to close. "Wha— yeah, thanks, Seth. We'll get 'em."

. . .

And we—or I should say, *they*, did get them.
On the next day Carson was dominant. He
worked efficiently with Nick, and the batters
they didn't strike out only managed laughable
bouncers to the infield. He carried a perfect
game into the fifth.

At bat we seemed to find our footing—
eventually. Their pitcher was a lefty with a
submarine delivery. His release point seemed
impossibly low. Our guys looked confused
and went down in order in the first. But
the novelty wore off abruptly in the second.
Sammy worked the count to three and one.
Then the pitcher left a fastball up, and Sammy
obligingly parked it in the seats.

"Man, his delivery looks weird, but his
stuff is weak," said Sammy as he took high
fives in the dugout.

And he was right. Once our guys started
focusing on the ball and not the pitcher's
hand, they all agreed that it was low 80s, and if
it moved at all, it tended to move up.

We tagged them for five more before their coach yanked the guy.

Meanwhile, Carson was steady—even with the lead, he was all business. On the bench, he huddled with Nick, talking through the next inning's batters.

Carson's perfect game was spoiled in the sixth when their number-four guy worked a ten-pitch walk. Then the next guy finally got around on one of Carson's fastballs after working a long at bat. He drilled it to right-center for a single. Darius managed to hold the other runner at third, but all of a sudden the Cubans had life.

"Pay attention Roadrunners. Look sharp. You've got the lead, but don't celebrate yet," Wash yelled from the top step of the dugout.

We'd all thought the Cuban coach was crazy when he had emptied his bullpen over the last six innings. He'd managed to keep the game from becoming a total blowout—it was still five to nothing in the sixth—but he'd used a lot of pitchers to do it. The way things had looked in the second inning, we'd all thought the same thing. Why not just pick a reliever and focus on the next game?

Question answered.

Wash sat back down next to me. "I'd do the same thing their coach is doing. When you've got hitters like their three and four guys, you'd be crazy to stop fighting. They're still in this ballgame." I barely caught what he said. No one had talked to me for what seemed like days.

Anyway, the cleanup hitter stepped in, and Carson went right at him. They say a really great hitter knows how to foul off otherwise unhittable strikes. This guy made me believe it. Carson was nailing his spots. His fastball looked as good to me as it had looked in the first. But after seven pitches it was still one ball, two strikes.

The cleanup guy's brother was breaking for second regularly, only to trot back when his twin fouled off another strike. He seemed to want to rattle Carson as much as he wanted to get to second. Plus, they'd yet to see Nick's arm—maybe they thought they had a chance for the steal.

They probably didn't under normal circumstances, but what seemed like Carson's fiftieth pitch to the same guy bounced on the plate. It was all Nick could do to keep it in front of him and hold the runner at third. The other guy took second without any trouble.

Now things got strategic. Carson and Nick didn't need a conference at the mound to decide their next move. Two pitches later, the bases were loaded.

Everyone was quiet. Nick wanted Carson to feel out the fifth hitter, their third baseman. He hadn't played in the first game. Carson followed the signs and worked the corners. The guy wouldn't chase, but he couldn't get good contact on the strikes. The count went full, and the guy fouled off a few more after that.

This was getting ridiculous. Coach sent a pitcher to warm up with the backup catcher. He didn't even look at me.

I tried to imagine myself in Carson's shoes. It wasn't hard—I'd been there yesterday, basically. I knew my vision would have gone tunnel. It would be only me and the batter. Whatever Nick showed, I knew I'd call on the high heat—the pitch that used to have only two outcomes.

Carson was different though. He was still aware of what was going on around the rest of the diamond.

I don't know if the guy on third was just getting ahead of himself or if he misunderstood his coaches. Whatever it was, he got a little too far down the line and Carson nailed him. It was a beautiful pickoff move, and the runner at third looked like he wanted to crawl under the base and die.

"Way to be in the game," Coach Harris cheered from the other end of the bench. A wave of high fives and pumped fists crashed over the rest of the Roadrunner bench. All I could seem to manage was to clap like I was watching a golf tournament.

With two outs, things were easier for Carson.

"You got him, baby! Ring him up! High heat! Finish him!" Shotaro boomed to Carson.

Wash gave Sho a look and cupped his hands like a megaphone. "Trust your defense, Carson."

Carson did exactly that. He threw a breaking ball that the batter chopped hard to short. It was a tough play, but Trip fielded the ball cleanly and his throw to first was perfect.

Jam over. It might as well have been game over. Cuba never threatened again, and we won five-zip.

# CHAPTER 22

*So now the series was even. That must have been a relief for you.*

Yeah. See, you've got to understand something about pitchers in that situation. I lost us the first game, singlehandedly. Every other guy on the team made a winning effort, but we still lost.

Carson managed to make my loss go away. The team has a clean slate, a second chance. But me? I go from loser to, at best, nonexistent.

My dad taught me that about tournaments back in KC.

"These weekend tournaments are brutal for pitchers, Seth," he said one time as we drove back from a game. "In some ways, it's harder than pro ball. I mean there, a pitcher loses a game, he's got another start in five days." He was wringing the steering wheel like he expected water to come out. "But these tournaments, you either win or the best you can hope for is for another guy to make the game you pitched disappear." He pulled his eyes away from the highway for a second to look at me. "So you've gotta win or you don't exist."

So, to answer your question, it's hard to feel relieved about not existing. Or I used to think it was.

# CHAPTER *23*

*We haven't talked about your father for a while. I understand he wasn't able to get the time off work to make the trip. Did you speak with him while you were in Cuba?*

No. We didn't talk. I mean, he called, eventually. After.

Anyway, there was web coverage of the game—not video, but written play-by-play, like on MLB.com if you're too cheap to pay. So he knew something went wrong. He texted—cheaper than calling—right after the game.

"Rough outing. What happened? Elbow OK? -DAD"

He always signs his texts—like they're emails or something.

Anyway, I wrote back: "Elbow OK. Just got a little off or whtevr. Srry."

"Don't be sorry. You'll get em next time. -DAD"

He wrote that, I remember. I read it. But all I could hear was "gotta win."

# CHAPTER 24

*So now tell me about the last game. You pitched, right?*

Eventually. I mean, yeah, I pitched. But I didn't start. I wasn't surprised. Coach was good about it too. He came to the hotel room I had to myself. I was rooming with Dave originally.

"You've got the best arm I've ever had the privilege of coaching, Seth. You're going to be an asset to this team. But I wouldn't be doing my job if I gave you the ball tomorrow." He was looking me straight in the eye. I appreciated that. It felt like no one had looked at me for two days. "I've known guys who've gotten stuck like you're stuck. Can't find the plate. Terrified they'll hit everybody. It takes time to fix it. And we will fix it. Just not tomorrow." He smacked me on the shoulder as he turned to leave. "Like I said, best arm I've coached."

Yep, some arm, that arm.

. . .

So Fumio started the game, and this time it was a game for the offense. Both offenses. Maybe it was the heat—all of a sudden Havana decided to show us how hot it could be. Whatever the reason, both teams scored in every inning. Both teams went through pitchers. But nobody could pull away. It was 8–8 when Sho got the Cubans to go one-two-three in the ninth.

All the players were tired now, and it showed. The tenth was sloppy for both sides, but no runs scored. Same deal in the eleventh, when Sho finally had to come out. He looked like he'd been pitching in a sauna.

Carson and I were the only pitchers left, so Carson finished the eleventh. We scored in the twelfth, and everyone got their hopes up. But Carson gave up a two-out, two-strike homer to tie the game. It was a good, honest pitch. The batter just anticipated and got lucky. To Carson's credit, he fanned the next guy.

"Tough break, Carson," Wash said as Carson came to the dugout, his head down. Wash put a hand on his shoulder. "Shake it off. We're still in this."

Carson crashed down on the bench. He didn't look devastated. He looked too tired and too hot for that. He looked like a melted crayon.

Coach had a tough call in the thirteenth. Not only was Carson worn out, but the team was essentially out of reserves. He had me and the backup catcher.

Coach and Wash huddled for a minute. They went over their options. Carson was batting fourth in the inning, so not only did he have to decide if Carson was too wastiredted to pitch, he might have to to decide if he was too wasted to hit.

After Wash and Coach finished, Wash came over and told me to loosen up and find my bat.

. . .

Fortunately, the Cubans weren't any better off for relievers than we were. Unfortunately, that meant I had no time to think in the on-deck circle. But maybe not thinking was good. Sammy and Darius slapped ground-ball singles. The Cuban infield was definitely getting heavy-legged. Donny worked a grueling at bat that finally ended with him foul-tipping strike three. It was just enough though to allow Sammy and Darius to pull off a double steal.

With runners on second and third, at least I didn't have to worry about a double-play ball if somehow I managed to make contact. If they even pitched to me.

It seemed like they would. The manager and the catcher spent a long time at the mound, talking into their hands. They didn't bother to hide it when they looked at me, though, waiting in the on-deck circle. And then the outfield moved in. *Way* in.

When Wash saw me staring at the mound instead of warming up, he called from the dugout, "Hey! Don't worry about anything out there, Seth. Just get the ball out of the infield. Your teammates will take care of the rest."

Nick stood next to Wash along the dugout railing. "You're a ballplayer, Seth. Forget the other stuff. Don't think. Just hit the ball like at Trip's pool," he yelled.

I smiled in spite of myself. And I really did intend to try. If not for myself, then for Nick and Wash. Heck, even for Carson.

The catcher set up behind the plate, and the ump called, "play ball." I stepped in and tried to forget.

I sat on the first pitch, a fastball without much zip, high and wide. The next one was inside, and I had to spin out of the way to avoid it. He'd gotten a little more on that one.

I stepped back in, ready for something in the zone.

In the instant he released it, I knew he'd made a mistake. It was almost a batting-practice pitch. But don't get carried away. I hadn't been a home-run hitter for a long time. Still, the ball sailed over the center fielder and landed where he would have been standing for anyone else in our lineup. Somewhere before I hit first base a wave of pity came over me for the pitcher. But as I cleared first and heard Sammy score, the next wave crashed. This time it was terror. I'd have to pitch with the game on the line.

# CHAPTER 25

*This is what I don't understand, Seth. I know what happened in that game. The Roadrunners won that game. You were the winning pitcher. You batted in the winning run. What I don't understand is why you did what you did after the game.*

[Long pause.]

Winning is a funny thing in baseball, I guess. On the score sheet I got a single and an RBI, but it was more the manager's mistake—

moving in the outfield so much and not walking me.

And then the bottom of the thirteenth? That had nothing to do with me. It was all Nick.

He grabbed me and said, "These guys are exhausted, Seth. Just like we are. Hard sinkers and splitters and fastballs on the corners. We can finish this."

Trip and the rest of the infield said basically the same thing as they took their positions behind me. I willed myself to believe that their banter was the sound of a second wind.

Maybe it was because we were in survival mode, or maybe it was because nobody wanted me to think about it, but I didn't give any thought to their batting order. At least not until their leadoff guy stepped up to the plate. The second hitter had been subbed out long ago, but other than that, it was the same first four who'd dismantled me two days before.

The guy stepped in and Nick crouched, smacking his glove and showing fastball low and away. I gave myself a moment to look at the batter. Definitely no mind games. He looked too tired and too focused. I was going to pitch and he was going to hit. OK.

He took my fastball for the ball it barely was. He fouled off a splitter and then refused to chase two outside fastballs.

Nick was working fast, trying to raise my tempo to keep me from thinking too much, and it worked. Kind of.

The batter chopped my next pitch hard to short. Even at full strength, it was a hard play to make. Trip had to range far to his right, grab the ball low, and make a hard throw to beat the runner. Nine times out of ten, Trip nails this guy.

Today, he was half a step behind. One on, no outs.

Nick jogged to the mound. "Right idea. Shake it off. You got a groundball. That's all we can ask. Those guys are going to make those plays for outs more often than not."

I got the grounder right away on the next batter. Nellie turned a hard one-hopper to third into a near double play. He nailed the runner at second, but Trip's throw was in the dirt and the runner was safe at first. Fatigue and heat were showing their effects.

Still, now it was one on, one out.

The third batter, their center fielder, was so familiar that I almost slipped back into slo-mo time again. Nick must have seen it coming. Because he smacked his glove and called time before I could deliver.

At the mound he just grabbed my jersey and said, "Throw it in there." He pointed to his glove. "Don't think about another freaking thing, Seth. I mean it." Then he gave me a little shove and spun back to home.

I'd never seen Nick really angry before, and maybe that's why he did it. It stopped me from going wherever I was going, at least.

He settled in, the batter stepped in, and I took the sign, came set, and threw. I heard the runner break for second, and my fastball stayed up more than I wanted. But it didn't matter. The batter must not have seen the pitch very well because he popped it straight up. Way, way up.

"Mine!" Nick screamed, and he camped under it a few feet outside the first baseline.

The batter didn't bother to run. And a second before Nick caught the ball, the batter looked at me. It was like he caught me staring—which he had, I guess. He just smirked and looked over at the on-deck circle, where his brother was taking the weights off his bat.

The ball smacked into Nick's glove.

One on, two outs. Their cleanup hitter now batting. It was seriously like something out a cheesy sports movie. Opportunity for redemption or whatever. Except I didn't seem to know my lines. It never occurred to me that I could strike out this guy—or any batter.

As he walked to the plate, it occurred to me that maybe Coach would call for an intentional walk. But that was ridiculous. No way would he move the winning runner into scoring position on purpose.

The batter stepped in, and Nick smacked his glove. He showed fastball inside, and I almost died.

I understood why. I'd been overworking the outside corner all inning. This guy had all his brother's power and a much better eye to go with it. No way could I get away with the same pitches.

I could almost see Nick deciding whether to call time. I could almost hear Coach calculating whether it would make more sense at this point to move me to left field and have anyone else face this guy. It seemed like I stood there forever.

In the end, I guess it was less terrifying to pitch than to stand. I managed an inside fastball, but it was well below Nick's glove and in the dirt. Nick blocked it, but it was enough for the runner to steal second.

1-0. Runner on second.

The ball was back in my glove, and Nick was showing inside fastball again. I really tried not to think.

This time I was more on target and the batter had to fight it off. Nick whipped around and tossed his helmet, but the ball was in the stands before I could get my hopes up.

The batter called time. He stepped out of the box and messed with his batting gloves—again. I guess he had one of those silly batting-glove routines some hitters have. All the time he was tugging on his gloves, he was staring at me. When he was finished, he tugged his helmet—one of the new ones from Carson's dad—and stepped back in.

As it turned out, he hadn't just screwed with my head.

. . .

When you lose your nerve—when you become a total head case like me—you think you're the only one. Everyone looks perfectly well-adjusted from the outside, while your mind is anywhere but in the game. It's so lonely.

But I guess I'm learning that's not quite true. Not everyone has it together. At least not the runner on second. I'm sure Nick noticed it way before I did—probably in the first game. This guy wasn't a crafty base stealer by any means. He wasn't particularly fast either. He just kind of ran wild on the base path. Maybe being unpredictable worked against some teams. Maybe it kept defenses off balance. So far, the runner had been lucky with us, but when I think about it, you could see that he made the base coaches nervous. The third-base coach in particular was staring at him like a dad trying to keep his three-year-old out of the cookie jar. And like a three-year-old, the runner wasn't really paying attention.

It was hard to believe, but I knew this guy might try to steal third. You've got to understand: making the third out at third base is a sin in baseball. And there was no reason for the guy to risk the steal. The cleanup hitter had been driving the ball all day. A good runner had a decent chance of scoring on a single. But still, the cues were unmistakable to anyone half paying attention.

Nick was totally on this and so was Nellie at third. I was trying very hard just to focus on Nick's sign and then his glove. So when he called for a pitch out, I just nodded, stretched, and for once, put the ball where I wanted.

Turns out a hard fastball was no problem as long as it was five feet away from the batter.

Nick's call was right. The runner broke for third, the third-base coach screamed "No, no, no!" but it was no contest. The coach spiked his cap in disgust before the ump called the runner out. Our bench cleared and mobbed Nick and Nellie

I just stood on the mound for a moment, staring at the batter. He shook his head. He looked like he wasn't completely surprised, but the disappointment was unmistakable.

And I get why now. When you play the game, you want to win or lose based on a real effort. If I had struck him out swinging, I know he would have been less disappointed. And if I had been the pitcher I was—before the surgery, before the headshot—I would have rather had him homer than to lose on some stupid mental error.

We both felt cheated. We both walked back to our dugouts alone.

# CHAPTER 26

*You won. Your team won. You played an important role in a close game. This is why it's hard to understand what you did next. Can you tell me what happened at the hotel?*

You don't get it. I was brought in to do one thing, and I failed at it completely. We still won because every other player pulled my dead weight.

It was worse to be the winner. Worse to have Carson slapping my back and saying

"Way to close 'em out." When Nick caught up to me in the dugout, it was all I could do to return his high five.

All the pressure. All the expectation. I failed. I wanted to disappear. I wanted to die.

# CHAPTER 27

*We've been dancing around what happened, Seth. I think it would be good if you told me what happened at the hotel.*

[Pause.]

You know, the very first thing I put up on my wall when we got to our new place in Vegas was a poster of Mariano Rivera. Do you know who he is? Probably the best high-pressure closer in the history of the game. His only job was to come in and win when the game was close. He literally never got the ball if there was no pressure.

I don't know what made me think of that.

[Pause.]

OK, OK. You asked about the hotel. Everyone was down by the pool. Nick told me to find a swimsuit and come down. It would be just like a party at Trip's, he said. I said I would find a suit. I went to my room.

It was so easy. In the bathroom, I just let a glass slip out of my hand. It broke into nice, big pieces. Sharp.

[Pause.]

I just cut my right arm, you know? People said that was a sign I wasn't serious, just cutting one wrist. But that's not it. I cut my right arm because in a weird way I thought it wouldn't hurt. Because it wasn't really mine.

[Pause.]

Crazy, right?

[End recording.]

# CHAPTER 28

From the *Las Vegas Sun*:
   Winning Pitcher Attempts Suicide
   By A. M. Amtaf (Associated Press)

Havana, Cuba. A young pitcher for
the elite under-17 travel baseball team
the Las Vegas Roadrunners attempted
to take his own life mere hours after
winning the decisive game in the
annual Goodwill Series. He remains

in stable condition at a Havana hospital.

The player, whose name is being withheld pending notification of family, was discovered alone in his hotel room by a concerned teammate. The teammate, Nick Cosimo, had been celebrating with the young pitcher in the hotel when the pitcher returned to his room.

"I got worried when he didn't come back down," said Cosimo, who, with the help of two coaches, managed to break down the pitcher's bathroom door. Emergency medical personnel were on the scene quickly.

"I don't understand why he did this," said Cosimo, "but whatever the reason, we're all pulling for him to come back. We're a team."

# ABOUT THE AUTHOR

Andrew Karre is a book editor and a lifelong sports fan and participant. He lives in St. Paul, Minnesota, with his wife and son.

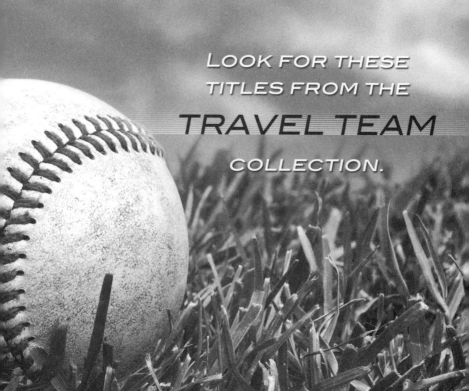

"The road to the pros
starts here."

LOOK FOR THESE
TITLES FROM THE

*TRAVEL TEAM*

COLLECTION.

# THE CATCH

When Danny makes "the catch," everyone seems interested in him. Girls text him, kids ask for autographs, and his highlight play even makes it on SportsCenter's Top Plays. A sports-gear executive tempts Danny with a big-money offer, and he decides to take advantage of his newfound fame. Danny agrees to wear the company's gear when he plays. But as his bank account gets bigger, so does his ego. Will Danny be able to keep his head in the game?

# POWER HITTER

Sammy Perez has to make it to the big leagues. After his teammate's career-ending injury, the Roadrunners decided to play in a wood bat tournament to protect their pitchers. And while Sammy used to be a hotheaded, hard-hitting, home-run machine, he's now stuck in the slump of his life. Sammy thinks the wood bats are causing the problem, but his dad suggests that maybe he's not strong enough. Is Sammy willing to break the law and sacrifice his health to get an edge by taking performance-enhancing drugs? Can Sammy break out of his slump in time to get noticed by major-league scouts?

# FORCED OUT

Zack Waddell's baseball IQ makes him one of the Roadrunners' most important players. When a new kid, Dustin, immediately takes their starting catcher's spot, Zack is puzzled. Dustin doesn't have the skills to be a starter. So Zack offers to help him with his swing in Dustin's swanky personal batting cages.

Zack accidentally overhears a conversation and figures out why Dustin is starting—and why the team is suddenly able to afford an expensive trip to a New York tournament. Will Zack's baseball instincts transfer off the field? Will the Roadrunners be able to stay focused when their team chemistry faces its greatest challenge yet?

# THE PROSPECT

Nick Cosimo eats, breathes, and lives baseball. He's a place-hitting catcher, with a cannon for an arm and a calculator for a brain. Thanks to his keen eye, Nick is able to pick apart his opponents, taking advantage of their weaknesses. His teammates and coaches rely on his good instincts between the white lines. But when Nick spots a scout in the stands, everything changes. Will Nick alter his game plan to impress the scout enough to get drafted? Or will Nick put the team before himself?

# OUT OF CONTROL

Carlos "Trip" Costas is a fiery shortstop with many talents and passions. His father is Julio Costas—yes, *the* Julio Costas, the famous singer. Unfortunately, Julio is also famous for being loud, controlling, and sometimes violent with Trip. Julio dreams of seeing his son play in the majors, but that's not what Trip wants.

When Trip decides to take a break from baseball to focus on his own music, his father loses his temper. He threatens to stop donating money to the team. Will the Roadrunners survive losing their biggest financial backer and their star shortstop? Will Trip have the courage to follow his dreams and not his father's?

# HIGH HEAT

Pitcher Seth Carter had Tommy John surgery on his elbow in hopes of being able to throw harder. Now his fastball cuts through batters like a 90 mph knife through butter. But one day, Seth's pitch gets away from him. The *clunk* of the ball on the batter's skull still haunts Seth in his sleep and on the field. His arm doesn't feel like part of his body anymore, and he goes from being the ace everybody wanted to the pitcher nobody trusts. With the biggest game of the year on the line, can Seth come through for the team?

# SOUTHSIDE HIGH

## ARE YOU A SURVIVOR?

check out all the books in the

## SURVIVING SOUTH SIDE

collection.

## Bad Deal

Fish hates having to take ADHD meds. They help him concentrate but also make him feel weird. So when a cute girl needs a boost to study for tests, Fish offers her one of his pills. Soon more kids want pills, and Fish likes the profits. To keep from running out, Fish finds a doctor who sells phony prescriptions. But suddenly the doctor is arrested. Fish realizes he needs to tell the truth. But will that cost him his friends?

## Recruited

Kadeem is a star quarterback for Southside High. He is thrilled when college scouts seek him out. One recruiter even introduces him to a college cheerleader and gives him money to have a good time. But then officials start to investigate illegal recruiting. Will Kadeem decide to help their investigation, even though it means the end of the good times? What will it do to his chances of playing in college?

## Benito Runs

Benito's father had been in Iraq for over a year. When he returns, Benito's family life is not the same. Dad suffers from PTSD—post-traumatic stress disorder—and yells constantly. Benito can't handle seeing his dad so crazy, so he decides to run away. Will Benny find a new life? Or will he learn how to deal with his dad—through good times and bad?

### PLAN B

Lucy has her life planned: She'll graduate and join her boyfriend at college in Austin. She'll become a Spanish teacher, and of course they'll get married. So there's no reason to wait, right? They try to be careful, but Lucy gets pregnant. Lucy's plan is gone. How will she make the most difficult decision of her life?

### BEATEN

Keah's a cheerleader and Ty's a football star, so they seem like the perfect couple. But when they have their first fight, Ty is beginning to scare Keah with his anger. Then after losing a game, Ty goes ballistic and hits Keah repeatedly. Ty is arrested for assault, but Keah still secretly meets up with Ty. How can Keah be with someone she's afraid of? What's worse—flinching every time your boyfriend gets angry or being alone?

### Shattered Star

Cassie is the best singer at Southside and dreams of being famous. She skips school to try out for a national talent competition. But her hopes sink when she sees the line. Then a talent agent shows up, and Cassie is flattered to hear she has "the look" he wants. Soon she is lying and missing rehearsal to meet with him. And he's asking her for more each time. How far will Cassie go for her shot at fame?